To Desi
Love from Grandpa Kent
and Granny Lu! Dec: 2021
We love you very much
xoxo.

Published by Familius™ LLC, www.familius.com

Familius books are available at special discounts for bulk purchases, whether for sales promotions or for family or corporate use. For more information, contact Familius Sales at 559-876-2170 or email orders@familius.com.

Library of Congress Control Number: 2020938223
ISBN 9781641702584 eISBN 9781641703659
KF 9781641703895 FE 9781641704137

Printed in China
Edited by Maggie Wickes and Brooke Jorden
Book and jacket design by Carlos Guerrero.

Images sourced or licensed from Shutterstock.

10 9 8 7 6 5 4 3 2 1

First Edition

12 Little Elves visit ALASKA

by TRISH MADSON

ILLUSTRATIONS BY
VALERIA DANILOVA

'Twas Christmas in Alaska
and 12 elves were sent
to see who was sleeping . . .

. . . away the elves went!

In each home was nestled
each girl and each boy,
while Last Frontier visions
brought everyone joy.

Sitka spruce trees glistened
with holiday lights,
and some Kodiak bears
started a big snowball fight.

In kayaks, the elves paddled
to Mendenhall Glacier.
The ice caves were formed
by elements in nature.

Atop Goose Creek Tower,
the Northern Lights were so bright.
The colors were brilliant
and lit up the night.

Seals on the Pribilof Islands
sang "Silent Night."
The elves sat and listened
with purest delight.

On the Iditarod Trail,
dogsleds were ready to race.
The elves were up cheering
all over the place.

King salmon were swimming in
Prince William Sound
as fishing boats got festive
and cruised all around.

The Santa Claus House made the
elves feel at home,
but they couldn't stay long
'cause they're headed to Nome.

The majestic Mount Denali
glistened with snow.
So the elves raced to the bottom—
ready, set, go!

At the Aurora Ice Museum,
they saw huge jousting knights
and lots of ice sculputres
all lit up with lights.

Next, Totem Bight State Historical Park.
The elves admired the carving at this famous landmark.

Good night, Alaska.
You're all fast asleep,
but there's just one more house
that the elves want to see . . .

Hurry to bed,
And shut your eyes tight.
Merry Christmas, dear Alaska.
12 elves say good night!